For Jared, with love
—J.M.W.

For my parents,
and for Mr. Witkowsky
—D.F.L.

Text copyright © 1993 by John Michael Williams
Illustrations copyright © 1993 by Diane Fontaine Levy
Wonder Books is an imprint of Durgan Michaels Publishing,
Boston Massachusetts
To order, call (617) 245–4629

ISBN 1–883084–01–6
Library of Congress Catalog Card Number 93–061122
Printed in the United States of America

10 9 8 7 6 5 4 3 2 1

First Printing

Illustrations: Oil on masonite   *Design:* Diane Levy
Text: 20/26 Garamond Three set on Macintosh
Printer: The Eusey Press   *Binder:* The Book Press
Paper: 80# Potlatch Karma

WONDERING WILLIAM
and the Sandman

By John Michael Williams

Illustrated by Diane Fontaine Levy

Wonder Books

BOSTON

1993

William wondered about so many things, he was called *Wondering William.*

He wondered why
water was wet.

He wondered why
snow was white.

He especially wondered about
the Sandman.

Some mornings he would
wake up with sand
in his eyes.

His mother told him,
"It's the Sandman.
He comes in the middle of
the night and sprinkles sand
in sleeping children's eyes."

Wondering William
wondered why
the Sandman did that.

Wondering William
wondered why
he never saw him.

And William wondered
how he could talk
to the Sandman.

So he wondered if he stayed awake but pretended he was sleeping, if maybe he could get to see him.

So he tried to stay awake.

But he could not stay awake.

Then he wondered if he wrote
the Sandman a letter asking
him to wake William up,
if maybe he would wake
him up.

So he wrote the Sandman
a letter. It said,

"Dear Sandman,

I would really like to meet
you. Would you please wake
me tonight when you come
to my house?

William"

But he did not wake him up.

Dear Santa,
I would really like

So he wondered if he left him brownies and milk, would he wake him up to say, "Thank you for the brownies and milk."

But he did not wake him up.

Now William wondered if maybe the Sandman wasn't nice. He became afraid!

So he wrote the Sandman another letter. It said,

"Dear Sandman,

I was wondering why you didn't wake me up when I wrote you a letter asking you to wake me up. I was also wondering why you didn't wake me up to say thank you for the brownies and milk I left for you. I was also wondering if you are a nice Sandman or a not-so-nice Sandman.

Your friend,
William"

William wondered if the Sandman would read this letter.

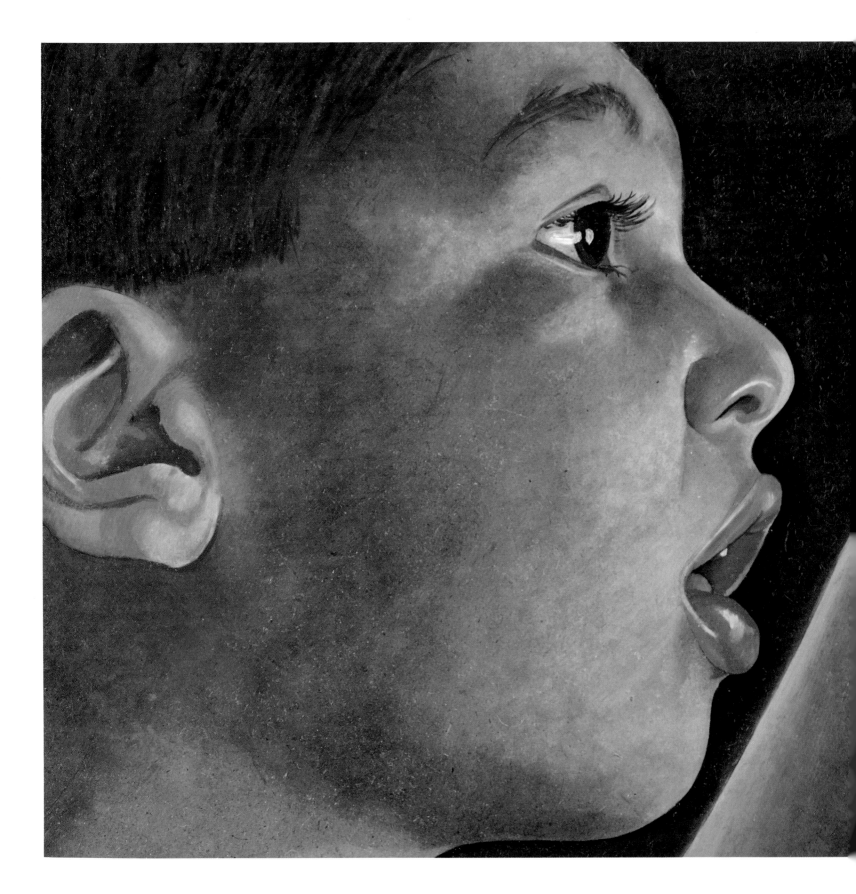

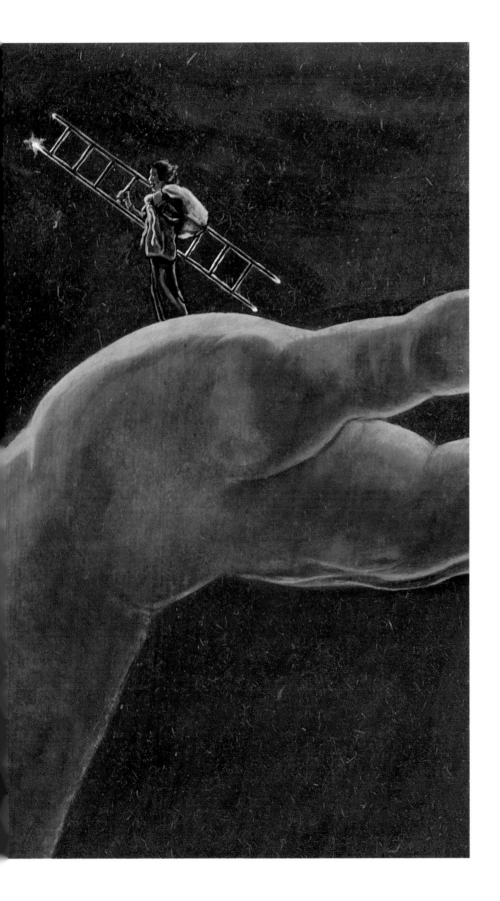

That night, as he was about to fall asleep, William heard someone calling his name. He opened his eyes. It was the Sandman!!! He looked very nice, indeed.

"You are special, William," the Sandman said, "because you are so curious. You are a very smart boy. And you'll keep getting even smarter because you're not afraid to ask questions. So I will tell you what you want to know.

"I sprinkle sand in people's eyes so they will sleep well and have pleasant dreams.

"While you are sleeping, I place my silver ladder against the bridge of your nose and reach into my sack for a pinch of sand. Then, *Whoosshh!* I sprinkle it into your eyes, and off I go, on to the next house. Now sleep well, and have sweet dreams."

The sandman winked, and away he went.

The next morning, William wondered if he had really talked to the Sandman. He wondered if it had all been a dream.

He climbed out of bed and noticed something bright and shiny lying on his pillow.

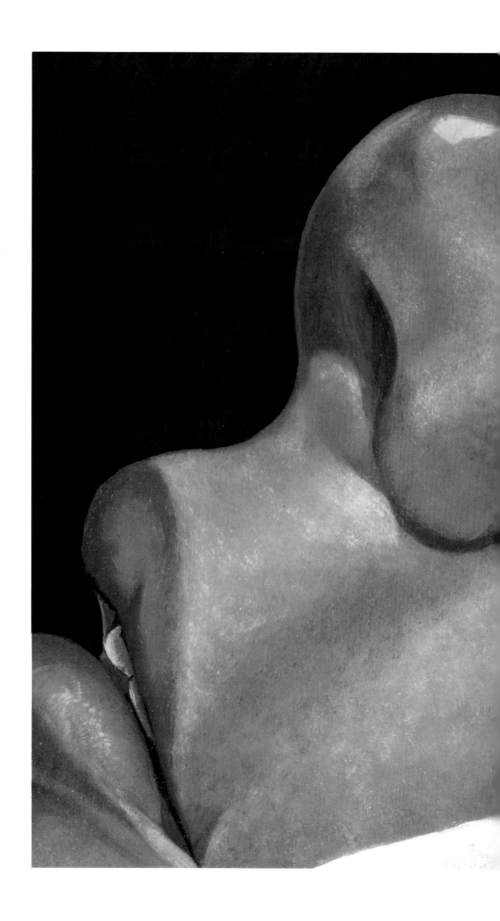

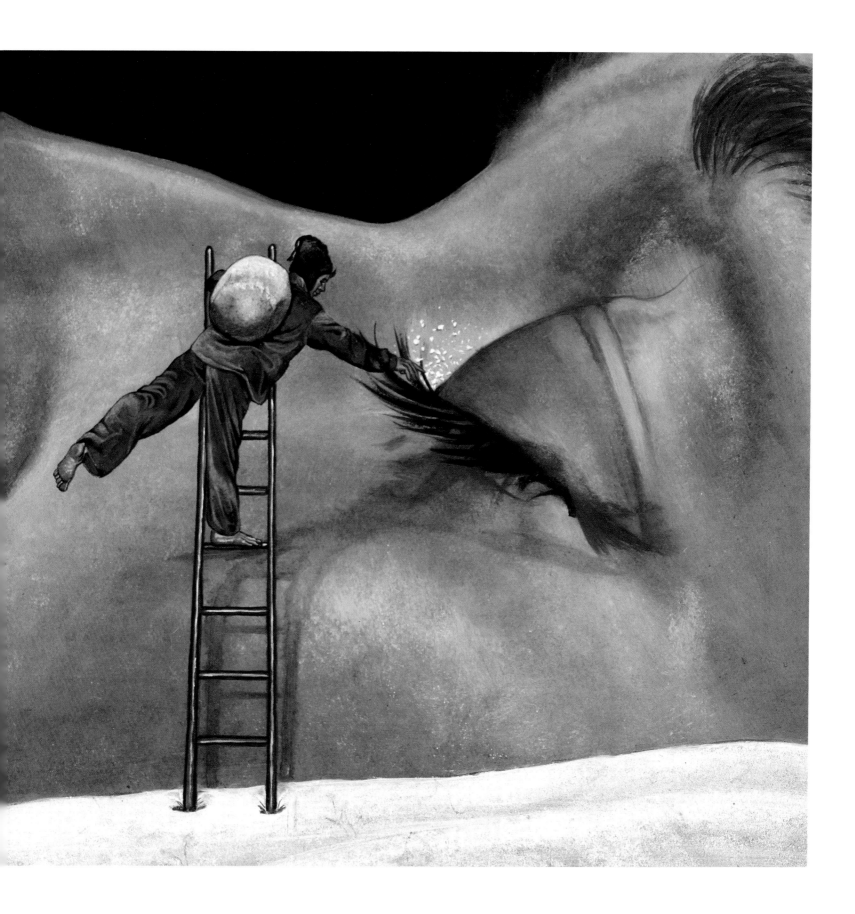

It was the Sandman's ladder!!!

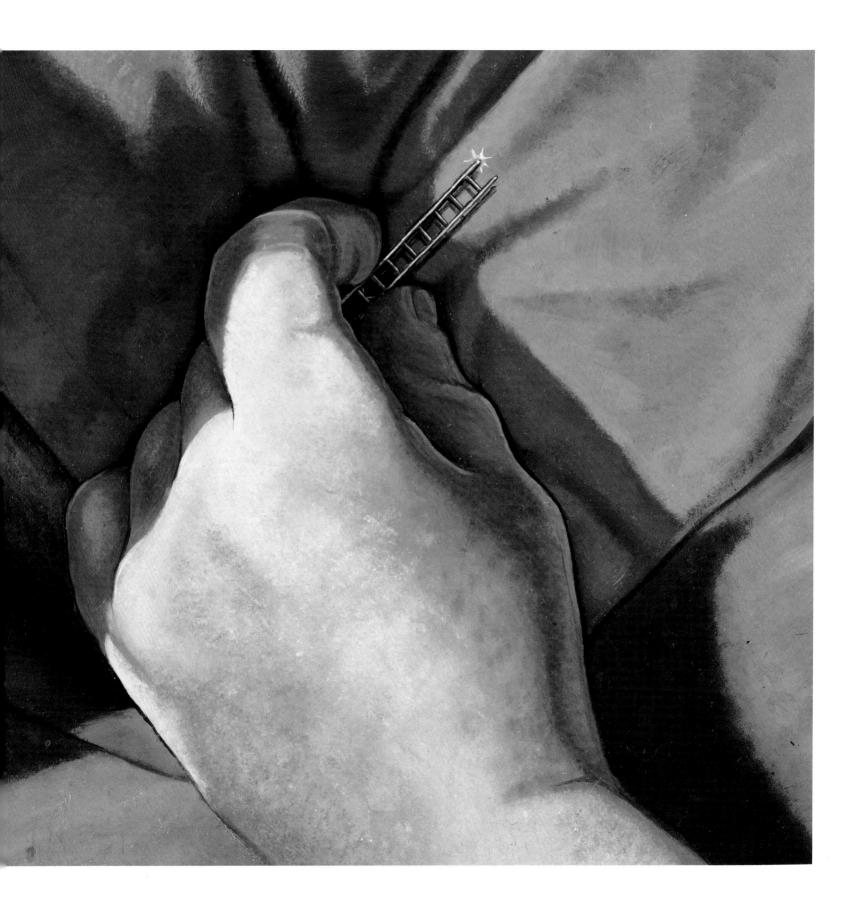

Wondering William
wondered no more.

At least, not about
the Sandman. . .